FOR THE LOVE OF LAXMI

Everyday Desi Biases and the Imprints They Leave

WRITTEN BY BIJAL SHAH

ILLUSTRATED BY ALEXA CARTER

You know, now your parents have to do things for him more. You are the older sister, so you have to be mature. If he wants something, he should get it first.

I love my brother, and I'll always give him everything, but why does Aunty think I wouldn't?

Do I bother my parents a lot?

Aunty is joking. You and your brother are equally important.

Aw, you are so good. Just make sure you smile next time!

I do smile when I'm at practice. I don't want to dance for guests all the time.

This is weird.

He went bowling with his friends yesterday and I didn't go! This is so embarrassing!

Mom! Why do I have to take him? It's a girls' sleepover!

Jenny has a younger sister. Rohit and Gia can play. Or Rohit will be bored alone at home.

MEET THE AUTHOR

Hi, I'm Bijal! I was born in India and raised in the US. I have always been fascinated by the dichotomy of being raised in these two cultures—the little bit of holding on, the little bit of assimilation—and everything in between; that's how Laxmi was born. Writing has always been a huge passion of mine, but I never thought my first book would be an illustrated book. But today, I couldn't love Laxmi more, and I hope you love her too.

☉ bijalshah

MEET THE ILLUSTRATOR

Hey there! I'm Alexa, and I've been drawing for as long as I can remember! I have always gotten the most joy from drawing to tell others' stories, and getting to help bring Laxmi to life has been one of my biggest joys yet!
🄞 puttheartincarter

To Kanudada, my grandfather.
Thank you for always seeing me.

Love always,
Your Mithudi